by Deborah Bruss

illustrated by Tiphanie Beeke

ARTHUR A. LEVINE BOOKS
An Imprint of Scholastic Press • New York

Library of Congress Cataloging-in-Publication Data
Bruss, Deborah.
Book! book! book! / by Deborah Bruss; pictures by Tiphanie Beeke
p. cm.
Summary: When the children go back to school, the animals on the farm are bored, so they go into the library in town trying to find something to do.
ISBN 0-439-13525-7
[1. Domestic animals–Fiction. 2. Animal sounds–Fiction. 3. Libraries–Fiction. 4. Books and reading–Fiction.]
I. Beeke, Tiphanie, ill. II. Title.
PZ7. B828755 Bo 2001
[Fic]–dc20 99-059758

10 9 8 7 6 5 4 3 2 1 01 02 03 04 05
Printed in Mexico 49
First Edition, May 2001

The illustrations in this book were created using watercolor and acrylic on 140-pound Arches paper.
The text type was set in 23-point Cloister Old Style.
Book design by Kristina Albertson

To my mother for her support
and my father for his humor
—D. B.

For Meike and Balder
With love
—T. B.

Down at the farm, all was well until . . .

. . . the children went back to school and the animals had nothing to do.

They had no rides to share, no tug-of-war to play, no one to scratch behind their ears or ruffle their feathers.

In the bright morning sun, the horse hung his head,

the cow complained,

and the goat grumbled.

The pig pouted,

the duck dozed off,

and the hen heaved a sigh.

Long about noon, with the sun high above the barnyard, the hen squawked, "I'm bored! And I'm heading to town to find something to do!"

The animals followed her down the road.

Library

"Look!" clucked the hen. "Happy faces. This must be the place we're looking for. I'll go in and see if I can find something to do."

"Neigh! Neigh!" whinnied the horse. "You're too small for such a big job. Leave it to me."

PUBLIC LIBRARY
open

The horse clip-clopped in. Politely he asked for something to do. But the librarian could not understand the horse. All she heard was, "**Neigh! Neigh!**" So the horse hung his head and clip-clopped out.

Next the cow plodded in. Politely she asked for something to do. But the librarian could not understand the cow.

All she heard was, **"Moo! Moo!"** So the cow complained and plodded out.

Now it was the goat's turn, and *he* trotted in. Politely he asked for something to do. But the librarian could not understand the goat. All she heard was, **"Baaah! Baaah!"** So the goat grumbled and trotted out again.

Slowly the pig ambled into the library.
Politely she asked for something to do.

But all the librarian heard was,
"Oink! Oink!" So the pig ambled out to tell her friends.

Up flapped the hen, and she announced, "I am going in, and no one is going to stop me!" Into the library she flapped.

"Book!" clucked the hen politely.

The librarian looked around and said, "What's that noise?"

"Book! BOOK!" clucked the hen.

The librarian scratched her head. “Who’s that?” she asked.

“Book! Book! BOOK!” clucked the hen quite clearly.

"Oh! Is this what you want?" asked the librarian,
and she handed the hen three books.

c
d

farm

Back at the farm, the horse, the cow, the goat, the pig, the duck, and the hen gathered around the books.

The barnyard was filled with **neighs, moos**, **baaahs**, ***oinks***, quacks, and *book-book-BOOKS*! Their sounds of delight lasted until sundown.

All the animals were happy, except . . .

. . . for the bullfrog. And do you know what he said?

“I already **read it!**
Read it, read it, read it. . . .”